This book is dedicated to my family
and everyone whose lives are touched
by the beautiful game
—ES

WordSong
An Imprint of Highlights
815 Church Street
Honesdale, Pennsylvania 18431
wordsongpoetry.com
Printed in China

ISBN: 978-1-62979-249-1
Library of Congress Control Number: 2018962504

First edition
10 9 8 7 6 5 4 3 2 1

The text is set in Avenir Book.
The titles are set in Rather Loud.
The illustrations are digital.

CONTENTS

THE BALL 5

INSTRUCTIONS FOR THE FIELD 6

UNIFORM DAY 7

A FEW WORDS FROM YOUR SHIN GUARD 8

A FEW WORDS FROM YOUR OTHER SHIN GUARD 9

WANT TO PLAY? 10

SATURDAY MORNING 11

INSTRUCTIONS TO: FIELD PLAYERS / THE GOALKEEPER 12

DRIBBLING 14

PASSING 15

DEFENDER 16

STRIKER 17

THE FANS 18

TEAMMATES 19

THE GOAL 20

APOLOGY 22

ACCEPTED 23

PEP TALK 24

THE GAME 26

THE HANDSHAKE 28

MORE! 30

GOOD DREAMS 31

A NOTE ABOUT POEM FORMS 32

THE BALL

Round
like the moon
sailing through space.
Round like an eye spotting
just the right place. Perfect for
trapping, tapping, and spinning.
Perfect for kicking, bending, and
winning. Scarred like a knee
after a fall. Our feet find
a world around
this ball.

INSTRUCTIONS FOR THE FIELD

Lie flat—
never slouch or slump.
Grow a thick, green beard—
never shave,
but keep it trim.
Wear the same striped suit
every day.
When it rains,
gulp greedily.
Catch us
when
we fall.

UNIFORM DAY

How about red? Red could have been right—
red like the eyes of a vampire at night
that freeze you in fear before the first bite.

Why, oh why, couldn't it be blue—
blue like a shark that knows what to do
when there's blood up ahead that smells brand new.

Even purple might have been okay—
purple like the bruise I earned that day
when the striker struck and I got in the way.

Anything would have been better than green—
green like a wobbly, soggy old bean.
I don't want to look cooked. I want to look mean.

A FEW WORDS FROM YOUR SHIN GUARD

Find me.
I'm under the bed.
Sure, I smell
like something dead,
but who cares?
Wear me.
Wear a pair of me.
Tuck me
in your sock,
and let's get out of here.
I want to be kicked.
It's why I exist.
I'm the shining armor
guarding your shin
while you run down the field
and go for the win.

A FEW WORDS FROM YOUR OTHER SHIN GUARD

Look.
I'm not there.
I'm not under your bed.
I'm not in your bag.
I'm not on your desk.

I'm here,
where you left me
after the game,
when you ran away
when it started to rain.

I'm here,
where you left me,
next to the field,
with an empty juice box
and an old orange peel.

WANT TO PLAY?

(One kid)

Hola.

Yo no hablo nada de Inglés.

No todavía.

Imagino que aprenderé en la escuela.
Mañana.

Mis padres dijeron que debería venir
acá y hacer amigos.

Cómo se juega al fútbol?

Soccer?

Si! Juguemos!

(Another kid)

Hola? That's Spanish, right?

I don't know any Spanish.

Not yet anyway.

I'm supposed to learn at school.
Next year.

My parents say Spanish is good to know,
so you can talk to more people
and make more friends.

Football?
I don't play football.
I play soccer.

Want to play?

Yes! Let's play!

10

SATURDAY MORNING

the grass
trembles at our feet—
game time

INSTRUCTIONS TO

FIELD PLAYERS

Your hands are
not the stars.
Your feet are.
Control the ball.
Let it go.
Never
catch it!
This is the most important rule!

THE GOALKEEPER

This is the most important rule:
Catch it!
Never
let it go!
Control the ball.
Your feet are
not the stars.
Your hands are.

DRIBBLING

I zig.
> I zag.

I stop.
> I start.

I dip.
> I drag.

I dodge.
> I dart.

I drive.
> I dash.

I break.
> I book.

I cruise.
> I crash.

I forgot
> to look.

PASSING

I'm running and I'm running and I'm running to attack.
When I see they've got the ball, I start running, running back.

I'm running and I'm running, and I'm seeing empty space.
I'm running and I'm running, and I'm getting into place.

I'm running and I'm running, and I've stomped each blade of grass.
I'm ready and I'm open. Why won't anybody pass?

DEFENDER

You think I'm a dog
asleep by the door,
my ears hanging
like the CLOSED sign
at the ice-cream store,
my eyes twisted shut
like the blinds in your room,
my head in a dream
world of rabbits.
See my shiny nose
grow wide.
See my ears shift
to the side.
I know you're coming
before you do.
You're the rabbit
I'm waiting for.

STRIKER

A shark,
slipping
through
the sea,
until
she smells
opportunity.
She sets
her course.
She sets
her soul
on one
essential
goal.

Quick
flick.

She scores.

THE FANS

I like it when my parents come.
I like that they are near.

But when they yell instructions,
I pretend that I can't hear.

TEAMMATES

We stretch
together.
We run
together.
We dribble
together.
We kick
together.
We attack
together.
We defend
together.
We cheer
together.
We groan
together.
Together,
we meet
our fate.

THE GOAL

Dear Goal,
I hear you calling me
to chip you a ball,
the same way my mouth
begs to catch a flying grape.
I wonder how
a soccer ball tastes,
and if you hate
the keeper who rejects
your favorite treat.
Maybe one day
your mouth will snap shut,
biting that annoying tongue.

APOLOGY

I got too mad.
I tried too hard.

I crossed the line.
I got a card.

ACCEPTED

I saw he was sorry.
I knew he felt bad.

I sat down beside him.
I didn't get mad.

PEP TALK

Sometimes,
when I'm frustrated,
I feel like a bit of dust
blowing across the field.
Dust can't
shoot with a weak foot,
or make a cross from the wing,
or break through a crowd with the ball.
But when I hear you say
Try again,
I know you think I can,
and I become the wind.

THE GAME

I imagine
the game
is in the hand
of a giant,
who tips
the field
back and forth,
rolling the ball
from one side
to the other,
bouncing it off
the players' shins
into the nets
at either end.

THE HANDSHAKE

I don't want to shake her hand.
She grabbed my shirt.
She pulled my shorts.
She pushed me out of bounds.

I don't want to shake her hand.
I want to grab.
I want to pull.
I want to push her out of line.

I don't want to shake her hand,
but I do
because I don't want to be
her.

MORE!

Win or lose,
when the game is through,
there's only one thing
we want to do!

We want to play soccer!
We're ready for more!

We don't need a ref,
a coach, or a fan.
With old friends or new,
there's only one plan!

We want to play soccer!
We always want more!

We don't mind the rain.
There's plenty of light.
We never get tired.
Who cares if it's night?

We want to play soccer!
Pass, shoot, score!

GOOD DREAMS

Sometimes at night
I lie in bed
and stick my feet up
over my head.

I toss my bear.
I kick him quick,
making a perfect
bicycle kick.

I watch bear fly,
spinning in air,
missing the bar
by one brown hair.

Upside down,
I settle the game.
Thousands of fans
sing my name.

I fall asleep
humming that song.
I kick that kick
the whole night long.